'**Watch out**, people, here they **come**,
They are the gang with the big bare **bum**.

Ring that bell,
CLANG CLANG CLANG,
That's why we call them the
BARE BUM GANG.

They're like something off the **telly**,
They're all bare and they're all **smelly**.'

D0320071

Also Available:

THE BARE BUM GANG
AND THE FOOTBALL FACE-OFF

Coming Soon:

THE BARE BUM GANG
AND THE VALLEY OF DOOM

www.barebumgang.com

THE BARE BUM GANG

battle the Dogsnatchers

ANTHONY McGOWAN

Illustrated by Frances Castle

RED FOX

THE BARE BUM GANG BATTLE THE DOGSNATCHERS
A RED FOX BOOK 978 1 862 30387 4

First published in Great Britain by Red Fox,
an imprint of Random House Children's Publishers UK
A Random House Group Company

This edition published 2008

5 7 9 10 8 6 4

The Random House Group Limited supports The Forest Stewardship
Council (FSC®), the leading international forest certification organisation.
Our books carrying the FSC label are printed on FSC® certified paper.
FSC is the only forest certification scheme endorsed by the leading
environmental organisations, including Greenpeace. Our
paper procurement policy can be found at
www.randomhouse.co.uk/environment

MIX
Paper from
responsible sources
FSC® C016897

Set in Bembo MT Schoolbook

Red Fox Books are published by Random House Children's Publishers UK
61–63 Uxbridge Road, London W5 5SA

www.randomhousechildrens.co.uk
www.randomhouse.co.uk

Addresses for companies within The Random House Group Limited can be
found at: www.randomhouse.co.uk/offices.htm

THE RANDOM HOUSE GROUP Limited Reg. No. 954009

A CIP catalogue record for this book is available from the British Library.

Printed and bound in Great Britain by Clays Ltd, St Ives PLC

To the BBG originals:
Graham Doran, Simon Morley
and Niall McGowan

Thanks also to Dylan and Declan
for lending Ray Quasar

No snakes were injured in the
writing of this book

Chapter One

A RUBBISH PRESENT

I could tell Dad was excited about something. His face was shining like a light bulb.

'I've got something for you, Ludo,' he said, looking at me and grinning.

I was with Mum in the kitchen. My baby sister, Ivy, was sitting in her high chair, making baby noises. She'd just learned how to make a raspberry sound, and that was her favourite. It went '*Ppprrrrraaaaaaaaaapppppp sssssssst*' and she was very proud of it. It was quite similar to the sound of her filling up her nappy, but not as soft and squelchy, or as smelly.

Dad was late and we'd finished dinner. It was fishcakes, peas and chips. Dad's dinner was on a plate in the oven, and it was all brown and shrivelled up, like it had been zapped by an alien death ray. Mum always burned Dad's dinner when he was late. I think she did it on purpose as a way of helping him to remember to get home early.

'A present?' I asked.

'Yes, sort of. It's just what you've always wanted.'

Mmmmm . . . There were lots of things I'd always wanted. A radio-controlled model helicopter, a Swiss Army knife, a crossbow, an air rifle, my own canoe, a robot that tidied my bedroom and did my homework and conquered my enemies using mind control. Any of those would have been good.

'What is it, Jim?' asked Mum. She didn't look like she thought it was going to be good. She looked like she thought it was going to be a disaster. Strange how mums always know these things.

'It's in the car. I'll go and get it.' Then Dad went out again.

Mum looked at me and shook her head.

The next bit of Dad I saw was his backside. He'd pushed the door open with it, and was trying to drag in something heavy attached to a rope. The thing he was pulling made a noise that sounded a bit like '*Grrrrrlllllaaaahrachshtrsshh*'.

It wasn't the sort of sound you wanted to hear, except maybe in a film where you like being scared. If I had to say what it sounded like, I'd say it sounded like a monster. A monster eating another monster.

Ivy said, '*Ppprrrrraaaaaaaaapppppsssssssst,*' which I think was her way of talking to the monster. In baby language it probably meant something like, 'I am the Leader of planet Earth. If you come in peace we will offer you the hand of friendship. But if it is war you seek, then planet Earth has powerful weapons and we will destroy you.'

Dad finally managed to pull the thing into the kitchen, and for a second I thought I was right. About the monster, I mean.

Mum screamed.

Ivy stopped going, '*Ppprrrrraaaaaaaaapppppp sssssssst,*' and started crying. Fine Leader of planet Earth *she* turned out to be.

'What is it?' shouted Mum.

'He's very friendly,' said Dad.

'Get it out of my kitchen!'

Dad didn't seem to hear. 'Had a bit of trouble with the old fellow. He didn't like being left in the car, and he . . . er . . . ate the gearstick. And part of the steering wheel. And . . . um . . . some of the seat. Quite a lot of the seat, actually.'

The thing he'd dragged into the kitchen wasn't a monster.

It was a dog.

The ugliest dog I'd ever seen. He had a short body, about the size of a microwave oven, and an enormous head as big as a toaster, and he had droopy, slobbering lips and only one and a half ears. His fur was black with brown splodges, and he had shiny pink gums.

This is my best drawing of him.

the dog Dad brougth In.

half an ear ⟶

some drool ⟶

pink gums

'Do you like him, Ludo?' Dad asked.

I quickly thought again about all the things I wanted, meaning the helicopter, etc., etc., and then I saw Dad's face, how excited he was, how much he wanted me to like him.

'Yeah, he's OK,' I said. 'What kind of dog is he anyway?'

'The man in the pub said he's a pedigree flugel hound.'

'There's no such thing,' said Mum.

'What's he called?' I asked, trying to stop the argument in its tracks.

'His name? Ah, well, there's a slight problem there. The man who gave him to me said he was called . . . well, it was a rude word.'

'What sort of rude word?' said Mum, sounding cross.

'Really quite rude.'

Dad mouthed something at Mum so I couldn't hear it. Then he said to me, 'We'll have to think of a new name for him.'

'No we won't,' said Mum, 'because he's not staying.'

'But I paid fifteen pounds for him!'

'You paid how much?' yelled Mum. 'He should have paid you!'

And then there was no stopping the argument. In the end, after all the shouting, it was decided that I could keep him for a month on trial, but that I had to pay for part of his food out of my pocket money. And I had to take him for a walk twice a day, which was all a bit unfair as I didn't even want him in the first place. And if he ate any more of the car or any part of the house then Mum would take him straight round to the vet's to be put to sleep.

The dog ate Dad's burned dinner and Dad had some cornflakes.

CHAPTER 2

RUDE WORDS

After the dog had finished Dad's fish cakes, chips and peas, Mum said I had to take him for his first walk. I called the rest of the Bare Bum Gang before I set off, but the only one who was allowed to come out to play was Noah, and he didn't want to because he was scared of dogs. So I went by myself to the field near the park, where you are allowed to walk your dog as long as you bring a bag for the you-know-what.

We didn't have a lead, just the rope that Dad had used. The dog pulled me all the way, as if he knew where he was going. It was like being dragged along by a tractor. Although he was strong, the dog didn't seem very vicious, which was a relief. But when it came to snuffling, this dog was the world champion. Everything on the way had to be snuffled - every stick, every stone, every lamppost. When he snuffled, as well as the snuffling noise he also made a wet *plapping* noise like an old man with no teeth eating an ice cream.

I'm not really scared of dogs, not like Noah is scared of dogs. He's scared of *all* dogs, even the friendly ones that wouldn't even *dream* of biting you. I think he might have had a bad experience when he was little. I'm only scared of the ones that definitely *do* bite you. And, frankly, anyone who's not scared of a dog that's actually biting them needs their head examined, as well as whichever part of them is being bitten — say, their leg or their bum.

But my dog didn't seem to be a biting dog, or not a biting-*people* dog, anyway, because he could have bitten me lots of times and he didn't.

When we got to the dog-poo field, Mrs Cake was the only person there. She had a dog called Trixie. Trixie was a Jack Russell terrier, about the size of a big rat, and she definitely *was* a biting dog. Trixie especially liked to bite children, because they're nice and easy to chew. So I *was* scared of her. Not as much as I'd be scared of a sabre-toothed tiger or a great white shark, but more than I'd be scared of, for example, some broken

glass or a medium-sized baboon that had escaped from the zoo.

Mrs Cake was also quite scary. Her hair was in a funny shape, and she carried an umbrella whether or not it was raining. In the Olden Days she'd probably have been burned as a witch. I don't think that would have been fair, and I'm glad we live in Modern Times, but you could sort of understand why they'd do it. It was probably why she had a dog rather than a cat, because if she'd had a cat, especially a black cat, then everyone would have said she was a witch for definite, rather than just as a maybe.

Well, I stood as far away from Mrs Cake and Trixie as possible. I kept my dog on his rope. But as soon as Trixie saw me she came running across the field, probably thinking she was in for a good old chase, with maybe a nice little bit of bum cheek to chew on at the end of it.

I felt my dog go tense at the end of the rope. I thought for a second that he was going to run away, adding being a coward to the list of things that made him a rubbish dog (ugly, smelly, stupid, only having one and a half ears, etc., etc.). But then I felt him pull forwards on the rope and I couldn't hold on. He ran straight towards Trixie making that same horrible growling noise he'd made when Dad first brought him to our house with an added bit of *plapping* and snuffling.

Before he reached the little rat, Trixie realized what was about to happen to her; she turned round very neatly and ran back to Mrs Cake, whimpering and whining. In fact, she didn't even stop when she reached Mrs Cake but shot straight past her. Mrs Cake shouted out, 'Trixie, *Trixie!* Come here, you naughty girl,' but that didn't make any difference. Then my dog trundled past her as well, and she hit him on the back with her umbrella, but he didn't even slow down.

Then Mrs Cake started shouting at my dog and she used some very rude words, and that was sort of funny – I mean, hearing an old lady use words like that – even though Mum says it's not clever or funny.

It was then that I decided what to call my dog. It was getting a bit silly just calling him 'my dog' all the time. So from now on he would be called Rude Word, or Rudy for short.

After the dogs had run off Mrs Cake shouted at me for a while, and I said sorry, although it wasn't my fault. What I really wanted to say was that I was glad that Trixie was getting a bit of her own medicine, but I didn't want to be rude to Mrs Cake because she had her umbrella at the ready, and anyway, it's wrong to be rude to old ladies, even if they might be witches.

Then Mrs Cake went to look for Trixie. A few minutes later Rude Word came back to me. He looked a bit guilty and was licking his lips.

'Good boy,' I said, and patted him.

Chapter 3

SOME NEW TRAPS, ETC., ETC.

The next day was Saturday, and straight after breakfast I brought my new dog down to the Gang den.

The den was in a tiny little wood near where we live. I thought Rudy would like the trees for weeing on, etc. He had a Weetabix for breakfast. So far, he seemed to be able to eat just about anything. Remember, he'd already eaten quite a lot of our car, and some fish cakes, chips and peas. Oh, and in the night he got up from his cardboard box and ate most of what was in the rubbish bin and also a pair of my dad's dirty underpants from out of the laundry basket.

By the time I got to the den Phillip, Noah, Jamie and Jennifer were already there.

Phillip is our Gang Admiral, which means he'll take charge of our navy when we finally get one. We usually call him The Moan, because he's always moaning.

Jennifer is The Moan's sister. We wouldn't normally let girls into our gang, especially sisters, but Jennifer was good at tae kwon do, which is like karate. It was her idea that we should be called the Bare Bum Gang, but I don't want to go into that now. It's enough to say that it was once something to be ashamed of, but that now it made us proud.

Noah is sort of my second in command, and also our Gang Doctor. The thing about Noah is that he's nice and wants everyone to be nice to each other and not fight too much or call each other bad names.

Jamie is our Gang General, because he's the best at fighting, apart from Jennifer. Jennifer

couldn't be the Gang General because her job was to be the Gang Girl, and that was enough work for one person.

The best thing about our gang is the gang den. Part of it is almost like a cave dug into the side of a hill, and another part sticks out at the front and that's how you get in. The entrance is cunningly disguised by the drooping branches of a weeping willow tree, and we'd made really good traps all around it to catch people who tried to invade us.

I'd recently invented a new kind of trap that I don't think had existed anywhere in the world before. I called it my balloon squirty-ink trap, and it was even better than the Smarties-tube fart bomb trap that used to be our top-of-the-range trap.

The balloon squirty-ink trap works like this. First you get a balloon and then you put some ink in it. This part can be quite messy, and it's probably best not to do it wearing your favourite clothes. If you've got an old *Spider-Man* costume or a pirate outfit that you don't like any more because it's for babies, you could wear that.

I think blue ink works best, but you can use any colour you have, say black, or red, or green, or purple. Then you take the outside part of a biro – I mean the bit that makes a tube when you take the refill out of it – and put it in the balloon hole. It won't fit very tightly, so you have to tie it on with some string, or use Sellotape.

The balloon part of the trap looks like this.

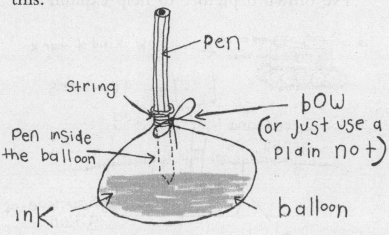

(The balloon looks a bit floppy because there isn't usually enough ink to fill it up.)

Then you put this whole apparatus into a hole you've dug specially (or you could use a hole you've just found lying around, or even one you dug before for some other reason, like burying a dead animal, or for making some other kind of trap). Next you put leaves and grass over the hole so that it's properly disguised. Then, when one of your enemies steps on it, his foot goes down into the hole and squashes the balloon, sending a big squirt of ink right up his leg!

I've drawn a picture to help explain it.

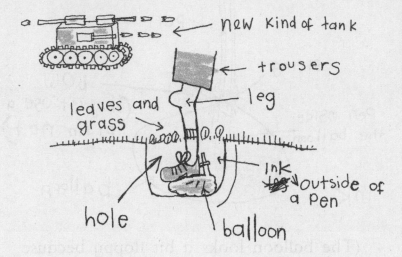

new kind of tank

trousers

leg

leaves and grass →

ink

outside of a pen

hole

balloon

I should say that the tank hasn't got anything to do with the trap. It was already on the piece of paper from when I'd drawn it before.

Chapter 4

GANG DOG, OR NOT GANG DOG? THAT IS THE QUESTION

'That is the ugliest dog I've ever seen,' said The Moan.

'I think he's sweet,' said Jennifer. I don't know if she really did think he was sweet or if she just wanted to disagree with The Moan, because he was her brother. 'What's his name?'

'He's called Rude Word, or Rudy, for short.'

They all laughed, and then when I told them why he was called that they laughed even more.

'Is he trained to attack?' asked Jamie, our Gang General.

'Probably,' I replied. 'He certainly attacked Trixie last night. She ran away. It was brilliant.'

They all cheered, except Noah. Noah was half in and half out of the den, ready to escape in case Rude Word turned savage.

'Does he bite?' he asked, looking nervous.

'I don't really know. He hasn't bitten *me*. But he might have bitten Trixie.'

'Shall we see if he likes it in the den?' said Jennifer.

'No way,' said Noah.

But all the rest of us thought it was a good idea. Rudy wasn't quite so keen, and we had to push and shove him through the door. He made a sort of growling noise, which sounded a bit as if he was saying 'rubbish' over and over. Actually, even in the short time that he'd been my dog, I'd noticed that Rudy quite often sounded like he was saying something. It was almost as if he used to know how to speak, but had now forgotten and only had a few words left, which annoyed him. One of his favourite words was 'ashtray'. He also sometimes said 'Saskatchewan', which is a place in Canada.

Finally we got him into the den. Noah was hiding in the corner being scared, and the first thing Rude Word did was to go and sit on top of him.

Noah didn't like that.

'He's sitting on me,' he said, in a sort of wailing voice. 'He's doing it with his bottom.'

'Well what else could he use for sitting on you?' said Jennifer.

'His bottom's all smelly.'

'He's got a clean bottom,' I said. 'In fact he's probably got the cleanest bottom of any of us. He licks it all the time.'

And then Rude Word began to lick Noah's

face. That really made Noah unhappy.

'I don't want dog-bottom-lick all over me,' he said, almost in tears.

Even though it was quite funny, I felt sorry for Noah and pulled Rudy off. The trouble was that then he went snuffling around the rest of the den, and his snuffle took him straight to our secret stash of sweets, buried in a shoe box under the floor. Rudy started to scrape away at the earth, with a big long line of drool dangling down from his mouth.

'Let's get him out of here,' I said, and it took all four of us, two pulling and two pushing, to do it. When we finally managed it, I threw a stick into the trees and told Rudy to go and fetch it. He looked at me like I was the stupid one, but then decided to wander off anyway, probably to test out the trees for weeing purposes. The rest of us went back into the den.

'Is he going to be our gang dog then?' Jamie asked.

'Well,' I replied, 'a lot of gangs have a gang dog. Like Timmy in the Famous Five.'

I'd been reading quite a lot of the Famous Five adventures, because I was worried that I was going to grow out of them soon, so I wanted to use them up.

'But that's a completely different sort of a dog,' said Noah, who was still in a huff. 'Timmy doesn't lick his bum and then lick your face. He finds treasure and rescues the others when they get locked into dungeons by the baddies.'

'What do the rest of you think?' I said to the gang.

Although I was Gang Leader, I always liked to find out what everyone wanted to do because that was only fair. If you never ask the Ordinary People what they think, then you're an Evil Dictator. I'm more of a Good King, like King Arthur or Queen Elizabeth I, even if she was a girl.

'I think a big scary gang dog would be quite cool to have,' said Jamie. 'And we can train it to destroy our enemies.'

'Yeah, I think it would be good too,' said The Moan. 'But if it eats our sweets, Ludo has to replace them.'

'I think he's quite nice,' said Jenny. 'But maybe instead of training him to attack our enemies, we should teach him not to sit on Noah, or lick his bum so much.'

That made us laugh, because it sounded like she meant that Rudy licked Noah's bum rather than his own.

'I don't think we can train him not to lick his bum,' I said. 'It's how dogs keep clean. It's instead of toilet paper for them. But every time he sits on Noah I'll tell him off and he'll soon learn. Is that OK, Noah?'

Noah said that it was, but he still looked like someone who'd been sat on by a smelly dog's bottom and wasn't happy about it.

'Shall we have an adventure then?' asked Jamie, after we'd sat around for a while.

We all agreed that having an adventure was a good idea, but then we got a bit stuck about exactly what kind of adventure. The Moan wanted us to use Rude Word to go hunting rabbits, but Noah said it was wrong to kill creatures for fun, and anyway we didn't know where there were any rabbits. I pointed out that Rude Word was such a stumpy dog he'd never catch the rabbits even if we found any. There was some talk about attacking pirates, cannibals, aliens, etc., etc., but that was just silly.

Then I had a brilliant idea.

Chapter 5

THE TREASURE HUNT

'Shall we see if Rude Word can find some treasure?'

I admit it was Noah who first mentioned how Timmy used to find treasure all the time for the Famous Five, but it was my idea to copy it. Anyway, it got their attention. Treasure is good for getting people's attention, because people like treasure more than almost anything.

'Yeah!' said everyone together.

'But how?' asked The Moan.

'Look,' I said, 'everyone knows that dogs are great for sniffing things out. You should have seen Rudy last night, snuffling away like crazy. It doesn't matter where you hide the biscuits, he'll find them. OK, so my plan is we let Rudy sniff a little bit of treasure, and then he'll be able to sniff out a whole lot of it. And we'll be as rich as emperors.'

'Which emperors?' Jamie asked suspiciously, as if I was trying to scam him out of some treasure by picking a rubbish emperor.

'Oh, I don't know. The emperors of China and Peru, probably.'

'Added together or separate?'

'Separate – there's no need to get greedy. Anyway, emperors don't like to be added together.'

He seemed happy enough with that.

'But what kind of treasure will we find?' Jennifer enquired. 'You don't get treasure just lying around the place, do you? Because, if you did, it would already have been discovered.'

'Well, it could be buried pirate treasure, or

golden coins left by the Romans. Anything like that.'

'There is one small problem,' said Noah.

That was bad news. Noah was usually on my side.

'What?'

'You said Rudy would need to sniff a little bit of treasure before he could find the great big load of treasure.'

'Yes?'

'Well, where are we going to get a little bit of treasure from? If we'd already found the big load of treasure, we could choose a little bit of it for Rudy to sniff, but then we wouldn't need him, because we'd already have it.'

Drat. He had a point. We were stuck.

It was Jamie who saved us, which was amazing, as I don't think he'd ever had an idea before, except for stuff like 'Oh, I'm hungry', or 'Oh, let's throw stones at that tree'.

'Money,' he said.

'That's clever!' said Jennifer.

'Of course,' I said. 'Money is a kind of treasure, so we let Rudy sniff some then he'll find some more.'

'So has anyone got any money then?' asked Noah.

For five minutes everyone patted their clothes and reached down into pockets. At the end of it we had three pennies and one two-pence.

'This is terrible,' said The Moan. 'If all we've got is rubbishy coppers, then that's what Rude Word will find. Even if he finds a whole chest full of pennies it won't be enough to buy anything cool.'

Then Jamie said: 'What about this?'

He held out something truly beautiful — a golden coin, exactly like the kind you'd find in a pirate's treasure chest.

'Is it real?'

'Yes, of course.'

'Real gold?'

'Real gold? Don't be stupid. Real *chocolate*. On the inside. It's the last one left over from Christmas.'

'That'll do,' I said. 'The outside is made of gold, isn't it, Jamie?'

'Yes, well, I suppose so.'

'That's fine. We only need it for the smell. So, my plan is, we let Rudy have a good big sniff and snuffle of the outside and then off he goes. And either he finds a treasure chest full of actual gold coins, or if we're really unlucky, he might just find a treasure chest full of gold chocolate coins, and everyone knows that the chocolate inside chocolate coins is the most delicious chocolate by a mile.'

'That plan is not completely useless,' said The Moan, which, for him, was like charging around and whooping and yelling and cheering and saying, 'Well done, you're a genius.'

At that moment Rudy came back into the den, having got bored with the outside. You could tell he'd arrived both by the smell and by the noise. The smell was a bit like manky bananas and the sound was like someone with a bad cold snorting back their runny bogeys, while also drinking a thick milkshake with a partly blocked straw.

So Jamie held out the coin for Rudy to sniff. He came over slowly on his fat legs. I mean Rudy, not Jamie. But Jamie also had quite fat legs. In fact in summer, when he wears shorts, his legs look like gigantic pink sausages.

Rudy didn't seem that interested to begin with, but then he went into hyper-snuffle mode.

'Yuck, he's licking it,' shouted Jamie. 'And he's got slobber all over my hand.'

'Well, that serves you right. You should have let me be in charge of the sniffing. I'd have done it properly.'

'Go on then,' he said, shoving the slimy coin into my hand.

I wiped the coin on my trousers to get rid of the dog drool. Then I showed it to Rude Word. He tried to jump up to eat it, but I grabbed his collar and made him sit. It was like fighting a bag of cement.

'Listen, boy,' I said, in a commanding voice, 'you have a very important mission.' He wagged his tail and looked like he was paying attention. 'OK, have another smell of this.'

I let him stick his nose against the coin. Unfortunately after he'd had his snuffle, he swallowed the whole coin, including the golden outside.

'Bad dog!' I said, and pulled my angry, angry face at him. I think that did the trick, because he looked quite sorry then.

'Now, boy,' I continued. 'Go find!' I pointed out of the door and away into the woods, in the general direction, I hoped, of treasure.

Rudy glanced back at me once and

shot off. Well, I suppose 'shot' makes him sound a bit faster than he really was, which was probably about as fast as a heavy wheelbarrow being pushed by an old lady with one leg.

Chapter 6

A GRUESOME DISCOVERY

'That dog actually looks like he might know what he's doing,' said The Moan, in an unusually un-moany way.

'Of course he does,' I said. 'He's a highly trained treasure dog.'

'We should probably follow him, in that case,' said Jenny.

Rudy had already disappeared into the trees, so we spread out to find him, pretending to be in the SAS. Pretending to be in the SAS was quite good fun for a while, but halfway through the dog-hunting mission I got a bit distracted. I found a nice whippy stick and started slicing the heads off a patch of nettles, which is one of my favourite things to do.

Then I heard a scream.

A girly scream.

That could only mean one thing – a girl was screaming. Or I suppose it could be a boy screaming like a girl. Either way, I had to help.

It probably meant someone was being attacked. They might have fallen into some quicksand, which made me really wish I'd brought some rope with me. I had my belt, which would have to do, even if it meant my trousers fell down while I was performing the rescue.

That was a chance I'd just have to take.

I ran towards the girly screaming sound, and found Jennifer standing in front of Rudy. She wasn't in the quicksand, which at first I was a bit disappointed about, but also quite relieved because I didn't want Jennifer to see me in my Teenage Mutant

Ninja Turtle underpants when my trousers fell down.

Rudy was looking a bit strange, just sort of standing there in front of a weird kind of a puddle. A puddle with chunks in.

'What are you screaming about?' I asked Jennifer. 'I thought something terrible was happening.'

I didn't mention the quicksand in case she thought I was silly.

'Something terrible *has* happened,' she said. 'Rudy's just been sick.'

'Oh,' I said, feeling a bit queasy myself. 'Well, don't worry. Dogs are sick quite a lot. It's one of the key facts about them.'

'But look at what's come out of him.'

'Isn't it just dog sick?'

'I SAID LOOK AT IT!'

Jenny was screaming now. I've heard that you're allowed to slap girls when they scream like that, as a way of calming them down. The trouble was that Jenny was really good at tae kwon do, and if I tried slapping

her she'd probably slap me back really hard,
and then push my face into the dog sick,
which is no one's idea of a picnic.

I looked.

'Is it a stick?'

'A stick?'

'A stick in the sick.'

'No. It's not a stick in the sick. It's a leg.
It came out of him when he was being sick.
He sicked it up.'

Then she made the noise of a dog being sick, in case I hadn't got the point.

'Don't be silly. Why would Rudy be eating a leg?'

'It's definitely a leg. It's covered in fluffy hair – look . . .'

There did seem to be some bits of hair on the sticky leg thing.

'And look at the colour of it,' Jennifer continued, her voice full of horror. For a second I thought about putting my arm around her, because it's what you're supposed to do when a girl is crying and needs comforting, or if you're afraid to slap her. But luckily I didn't, because just then I noticed that the rest of the Gang were there. They'd obviously homed in on the girly scream.

Jennifer quickly told them about the gruesome find, and they gathered round the doggy sick.

'It's a sort of browny colour,' said The Moan.

'Trixie's got one brown leg like that,' said Noah.

We all looked at each other, except for Rude Word, who had wandered away from the sick and was staring into the distance with an embarrassed sort of look on his ugly mug.

Chapter 7

Funeral Rites

'Oh heck,' said Jennifer, her eyes wide with horror. 'Do you think Rude Word has really eaten Trixie, and that bit of leg is all that's left?'

I didn't know what to say. I'd already had a silly, jokey thought about Rudy eating Trixie, and now it looked like it might have come true.

'That is *so* gross,' said Jamie.

He was usually in favour of gross stuff, such as eating his bogeys, or scratching his bottom and then smelling his finger.

'But at least we won't get chased by

Trixie any more when we play football,' said Noah, looking on the bright side.

'No, I don't believe it,' I said. 'He may be ugly and smelly and not very bright, but he wouldn't eat another dog. He's not a cannibal. He probably just wanted Trixie to be his girlfriend.'

'Dogs don't have girlfriends,' said Jamie.

'Yes they do,' said Jennifer, 'and they get married sometimes too. Everyone knows that.'

'Yuck,' said The Moan. 'That's worse than eating her.'

'We're getting off the point,' I said. 'It probably isn't even Trixie. I mean, Trixie's leg. I think it might be a hairy stick of some kind.'

'Yeah,' said The Moan. 'A stick from the famous hairy tree.'

'No need to be sarcastic,' said Noah.

'And even if it is Trixie's leg, how do we know that Rude Word has eaten the rest of her?'

'What do you mean? Are you saying that Trixie might have just dropped one of her legs, and gone off hobbling about on three instead of four? And then Rude Word just happened to find the one that Trixie dropped and said, "Oh look, a spare leg, that's lucky, I think I'll eat that"?'

That was The Moan, of course, continuing to be sarcastic, which is the lowest form of humour apart from farting in church.

'No,' I replied, keeping my voice nice and even, 'I mean, maybe something else killed Trixie, and ate most of her, except for one leg.'

'Like what?' asked Noah.

'Maybe an eagle?'

'There aren't any eagles around here. And anyway, why would it leave one leg?' said Jennifer.

'Maybe it was full. Quite often I can't finish all my shepherds' pie,' said Noah, backing me up, although I could tell his heart wasn't really in it.

'It could have been a fox,' I said, because I was never really convinced by the eagle idea. 'Or there might be an escaped black panther. I read somewhere that leopards like to eat dogs, and a black panther isn't a separate species at all, just a kind of leopard, which people don't realize. Yeah, that's probably it.'

We all thought about that for a minute. About being eaten by an escaped black panther, I mean. And nothing being left of us except for one leg. Or four legs, if you counted us all together. I suddenly regretted having brought up panthers. I knew that, as Leader, it was my job to cheer everyone up.

'Look, let's stop thinking about whatever it is that used to own the leg that Rudy's eating, and whatever it is that ate the rest of it.'

'Eh?' said Jamie. And I suppose you could understand why.

'I think we should have a funeral for Trixie,' said Noah.

'Good idea,' I said. 'We definitely ought to bury her. I mean, bury what's left of her.'

'You mean bury her leg?' said Jennifer.

'Yes, it's what she would have wanted.'

So we gathered around the leg, even Rudy, who was being quite well behaved, except for a small amount of bottom-licking. None of us wanted to look at the remains too closely. I tried to imagine the rest of Trixie still attached to it, and I looked at the imaginary parts and not the chewed and sicked-up bit.

I found a stick and scraped a hole in the ground. Not a very deep hole, because it's quite hard digging a hole with a stick. When the hole was finished, I used the stick to poke the leg into the hole. Then I used the stick to scrape the soil back over the leg.

Sticks are brilliant. You can use them for all kinds of things – for example, throwing, poking, stabbing, sharpening, slashing, etc., etc.

'Do you think we should say something?'

said Noah, once I'd stopped poking about with the stick. 'I mean, some nice words about Trixie.'

I nodded. Everyone bowed their heads and I began.

'Oh Lord, Trixie was quite a good doggie, even if she used to chase us around the football pitch all the time and bite us whenever she could. Please look after her in heaven, and take her for walks. If you are busy, then one of the angels can take her. Maybe as a special treat you could let Trixie chase some of the bad people down in you-know-where as part of their punishment – for example, Hitler, Attila the Hun, and that horrid one from *Pop Idol* who tells girls that they can't sing and are too fat. And please forgive whoever it was that ate the rest of Trixie apart from this leg which we are burying now, because they probably didn't mean any harm and it was just an accident. Amen.'

'Amen,' said everyone else.

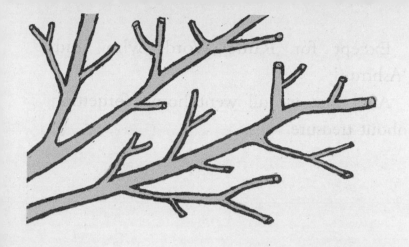

Except for Rude Word, who said, 'Ashtray.'

After that we all went home, forgetting about treasure.

Chapter 8

THE MYSTERY DEEPENS

When we got home, Mum said she'd decided that Rude Word had to sleep in the garage where there was nothing for him to chew up except the lawnmower and some bricks. Dad had made a sort of bed for him out of the baby bath, which my little sister Ivy didn't need any more because now she gets her stinky bum washed in the ordinary bath, like the rest of us.

Rudy had to wait in the garage until we'd finished our tea. Mum said that the best thing for him to have for dinner was our left-overs. I was pleased because his dinner didn't have to come out of my pocket money. You shouldn't feel sorry for him because there were always plenty of leftovers in our house: Ivy didn't eat anything green or orange, and I didn't eat anything that's sloppy or has sauce on it, or that's been on the same plate as anything with sauce on it. Sauce includes gravy, but not vinegar, because I like that.

I didn't mention about Rudy maybe eating Trixie, partly because he probably didn't, but mainly because they'd get rid of him for definite if they thought he had, and I'd grown quite fond of the ugly brute.

But at tea time my dad said something to my mum that made my blood run cold.

'Have you heard about Mrs Cake's little dog?'

'No, what about it?'

'Disappeared.'

'Really? That's funny.'

'Why?'

'Well, the postman told me this morning

that the King Charles spaniel that always used to bark at him at number seven has run away. He said the Johnsons were very upset about it, but it's the best news he's had all year.'

'Strange them both disappearing,' said Mum. 'I wonder if they're linked?'

'Well,' said Dad, 'they were both pedigrees, so perhaps they were kidnapped by dogsnatchers.'

Mum laughed.

And then she stopped laughing, and a quite complicated expression came over her face, as if she'd just thought of a brilliant plan but didn't want anyone else to know about it.

Luckily Rude Word wasn't around to hear all this. He was still trying out his new bed in the garage.

I had trouble sleeping that night. I had a lot on my mind. Mainly, of course, it was the whole thing about Rude Word and whether or not he had gobbled up Trixie.

Even worse than that, if those other two dogs had disappeared, then maybe Rudy had eaten them as well. That made him a serial cannibal dog, which is just about the worst, most embarrassing kind of dog there is, after a sausage dog.

Finally, when I was nearly asleep, I heard a snuffly, growly sound outside. I went to the window and looked out. Mum was dragging Rude Word along by his rope. When they reached the gate, she tied him to the post and then hung some sort of sign over it. Then she patted Rudy and went back to the garage and got his bed and blanket. I didn't think much about it because I was tired by then, and I soon fell asleep, dreaming about dogs and trousers and being kissed by Mum.

When I left for school in the morning, Rude Word was still there, asleep in his bed.

The sign said:

BEWARE! — VERY EXPENSIVE DOG

I was quite pleased that Rudy had a job at last, even if it seemed a funny way to scare people off.

The next day was Saturday. I tried to teach Rude Word some tricks, but he spent most of the day licking his bottom. Mum made him eat his supper in the garden. He had three fried eggs and some cold baked beans.

The sign was still on the gate. Dad gave Mum a funny look when he saw it, but he didn't say anything.

It rained on Sunday so nothing happened apart from more bum licking.

School on Monday was not very nice. Some of the other children were talking about the pet dogs that had gone missing. We tried to ignore it, but I think the Bare Bum Gang were all secretly afraid in case it turned out to be our fault and we got blamed and everyone hated us.

But that evening things took a turn for the better, at last, even though at first it seemed as though they'd got worse.

Chapter 9

MALCOLM (MY TEDDY)

My numeracy homework was measuring things. We had to measure an object in every room in the house. I'd measured some forks in the kitchen, the telly in the living room, a toothbrush in the bathroom, and a toilet roll in the loo.

So next I was looking for something to measure in my bedroom. I thought I'd try my old teddy, Malcolm. I hadn't really played with Malcolm for a long time, because I didn't need him to look after me any more now that I was old.

I felt a bit guilty about not playing with

him, which is why I thought I'd measure him, to make him feel wanted again. But now I couldn't find him. I looked under the bed and on the shelves and in my toy box.

'Mum, where's Malcolm?' I yelled downstairs.

Before she answered, who should wander in but Rude Word. There was something in his mouth. I knew what it was. Or rather, *who* it was.

In case you aren't very good at guessing, I'll tell you – it was my poor old bear!

'Bad dog!' I shouted, and tried to pull Malcolm from the Jaws of Death. Rude Word pulled back. I've already said how strong he was, and he certainly wasn't the kind of dog who'd give up a tasty meal – even one made mainly of fluff and hair – so you can probably imagine what happed next:

RRRRRIIIIIIIIIIIIIIIIIPPPPPPPPPPPP!

Rude Word had the head end.

I had the back end.

In between there was nothing.

That was it. I lost my temper and started really screaming at him. I used all the bad words I know, such as stupid, fat, nasty, idiot, smelly, ugly, smelly, fat, stupid, idiot, etc., etc. That seemed to work, because Rude Word sat down and spat out the parts of Malcolm he was chewing.

I don't want to come across as a baby, but I got quite emotional then. Malcolm had been a faithful bear, and had fought off all kinds of monsters that would otherwise have got me when I was asleep, including dragons, vultures, Gaseous Aliens from Uranus, vampires and werewolves. Once when I had chicken pox he stayed up all night to make sure I didn't die.

And so I cried – quite a lot, really. Rude Word came over and sat on me, which I think was his way of saying sorry, but I pushed him away. Then Mum came in. She'd heard me crying, which means I must have been quite loud, which is a bit embarrassing. It was lucky there was no one important around to hear. I told Mum what had happened, and she said not to worry, because she could sew Malcolm together and make him all well again. She dried my eyes with some clean underpants from my underpant drawer, and I felt a bit better.

'Let's find all the pieces,' said Mum.

'What do you mean?' I said. 'Here's the top and here's the bottom.'

'But what about the other leg?'

That's when I saw it.

I mean, *didn't* see it.

Of course, Malcolm.

Two arms. One leg.

One brown leg.

He was supposed to have two.

And I knew where the second one was.

Chapter 10

THE NEW SUSPECT

It was raining again the next day, so at school we had to stay indoors at break and play with the rubbish Lego they have. You would have thought it was impossible to break Lego, but half of the bricks have been chewed so they don't snap together properly. So, if you built a really good space station, or even a new type of tank, there'd be a good chance it would just fall apart, like it was made of dried bogeys and ear wax.

At least being inside gave us a chance to talk things over without getting hit by a football. We were all there, apart from Jennifer, who was playing with the girls somewhere else, probably doing girl things, such as skipping, talking, hair-brushing and being mean about other girls, etc., etc.

Naturally we talked about Rude Word. I couldn't wait to tell them about Malcolm's leg.

'Don't you see?' I explained to the Gang. 'It means that Rudy didn't eat Trixie.'

'Actually,' said Noah, 'it only proves that Rudy ate Malcolm's leg, not that he didn't also eat Trixie.'

'That's just stupid,' I said. 'Are you saying that Rudy eats bears and dogs? Nothing eats bears *and* dogs. Everyone knows that.'

'Well, whatever he ate, I say he's voted out of the Bare Bum Gang,' said The Moan, kicking things off in his usual cheery way. (That's me being sarcastic, this time, in case you didn't notice.)

'You can't vote him out by yourself,' I said.

'What about you?' said The Moan, looking at Noah.

Noah started to take a lot of notice of his fingernails.

'Jamie, what do you think?' continued The Moan. Jamie was trying to separate two bits of Lego with his teeth. 'You agree with me, don't you?'

Jamie said something like, 'Oogaggomp,' because of the Lego in his mouth.

'See!' said The Moan. 'Let's face it, he's a useless dog, even if he isn't a cannibal, or a teddy-bear-eater. He's never going to find any treasure. He doesn't even fetch sticks, or roll over, or play dead. What we need is a decent gang pet, one like Declan and Dylan have.'

Declan was in our class and Dylan was

his older brother, who went to big school. Declan wasn't in our gang. He was in a different gang. They called themselves The Commandos, but they mainly played card games like Pokémon and Yu-Gi-Oh! that have rules so complicated that nobody really understands them.

The Commandos weren't our friends or our enemies. It was a bit like the United Kingdom and, I don't know, say Peru or Greenland. We just didn't have much to do with them.

Actually, of all The Commandos, Declan was the one we talked to the most. He was a bit crazy and was always getting into trouble for not sitting still when Mrs Walsh was taking register, or for yelling out, 'I'M A BANANA, I'M A BANANA,' at the top of his voice during quiet time. And because he was a bit crazy, everyone liked him. Well, not really Mrs Walsh, but she didn't matter.

Another reason everyone liked Declan was because of his pet. And even I had to admit that it was probably the coolest pet in the world.

'Yeah,' said Jamie, freeing himself from his Lego, 'a snake!'

'Not just a snake, but a *giant* snake – a python,' said The Moan, rubbing it in.

'Actually I think it's a boa constrictor,' said Noah, but that didn't really help me as 'boa constrictor' sounds even more cool than 'python'. And both of them sounded way better than Rude Word.

The snake even had a cool name. It was called Ray Quasar.

'It's brilliant,' continued The Moan. 'They feed it on live animals. Rats. Anything really. But it has to be alive. You can't just give it dog food or sausages.'

And that's when it hit me.

'Quick, Noah!' I yelled. 'Go and get me a pencil and some paper.'

'Right,' I said when I had the equipment sorted out. 'I think I've discovered what happened.'

There were some gasps then, although part of it was just Noah having a mild asthma attack because of all the dust in the bottom of the Lego bucket.

'Think about it, everyone. Animals — *warm-blooded* animals, that is — have been going missing and poor old Rude Word has got the blame. Well, now we know he's innocent, but there is, in fact, a vicious predator on the loose — one that has a well-known taste for *warm-blooded* animals.'

I could see from their eyes that they were beginning to get it too.

'What?' said Jamie. 'Are you saying that there actually is a real black panther in the park?'

'No,' I said patiently, 'it's Declan's python.'

'Or boa constrictor,' chipped in Noah.

'What a load of rubbish,' said The Moan. 'How can a pet snake eat three dogs?'

'I'll show you how,' I answered. I sketched and explained at the same time, which was quite hard because I always do my best drawing with my tongue sticking out of the corner of my mouth.

'I remember reading a book and there was a picture of a python, or maybe a boa constrictor, and it had just eaten an elephant.'

'ELEPHANT!' they all yelled.

'Yes,' I continued. 'And you could see it inside the snake. I can't remember how, exactly. I suppose it was probably a drawing and not a photograph. Yes, that's it, it was like one of those cross-sections you see, but instead of a battleship or a jumbo jet, it was of an elephant eaten by a snake.'

'What is he on about?' said Jamie to The Moan.

The Moan shrugged his shoulders.

'And it looked *exactly like this*,' I said triumphantly, holding up my drawing of the other drawing.

And this is it, although I've smartened it up a bit on my own since then, so it wasn't quite as good as this to begin with and it didn't originally have the poo coming out of it — that was Jamie. I find it highly un-likely that an elephant inside a snake is going to be in a fit state to go to the toilet.

'No way could that be real,' said The Moan.

'It was in the book,' I said. 'And things in books are always true. It looked exactly like this.'

Then there was a really big row. In the end Noah went and asked Mrs Walsh. She said that she didn't think there was a snake big enough to eat an elephant. Then she helped us go on the Internet, and we found a film of an anaconda, which is the biggest snake in the world, eating a pig. Sadly, she wouldn't let us actually watch the film because she said it would be too gross and scary.

So then I went back to my pens and paper and drew a picture of the pig inside the snake, which everyone, even The Moan, said was really good.

This is the picture:

We all agreed that a pig inside a snake could easily happen.

'And a pig,' I said, 'is definitely bigger than a dog.'

Then I drew a picture of Trixie inside the snake.

'I think this proves for an absolute fact that Trixie is the victim of a snake.'

'I don't think you've completely proved it,' said Noah. 'I mean, I admit that it's very likely, but very likely isn't the same as proved. I think we need to do some more investigating.'

'Mmm,' I said. 'Maybe you're right. Tonight we go to Declan's house to . . . Oh, drat, Noah, what's that really good word you use when the police have captured a criminal and they ask them really hard questions?'

'Interrogate.'

'Precisely. Tonight we interrogate the python!'

'Or boa constrictor.'

Chapter 11

RAY QUASAR

I didn't talk about the mission any more then, because I knew that this was a job for an Elite Force, the best of the best, which probably wouldn't include The Moan (because of the moaning) or Jamie (because of him being slightly thick).

So my Elite Force was going to be me, Noah, who always said that he wasn't afraid of snakes, and Jenny, who wasn't afraid of anything.

At tea time my mum and dad were talking about the mysterious disappearances again. There had been more of them, and it wasn't only dogs now that had gone missing. A Persian cat called Fatty had vanished from a house on the new estate. And a parrot called Potty had gone too, leaving an empty cage behind.

It was obvious now what was happening. Ray Quasar was working his evil way through all the animals in town, and would soon move on to humans, probably beginning with the babies, before swallowing the children and finishing up with the adults, as a kind of dessert.

By my calculations, within three weeks there would be nothing left alive in town except for one bloated python. Or boa constrictor.

I telephoned Noah after tea.

'There have been developments. We're meeting at Declan's house at nineteen hundred hours o'clock.'

I wouldn't tell him any more. Then I phoned Jennifer and explained all about Ray Quasar. She was very pleased to have been selected for the mission, especially as her brother, The Moan, hadn't been.

Declan answered the door.

'Hello. What do you want?'

'We've come to talk to you,' I said, trying to sound like a detective or a secret agent. 'And your snake.'

'You want to talk to Ray Quasar? I thought it was only Harry Potter who could speak snake language.'

Then Jenny pushed past me. 'Look,' she said, 'we just want to find out some things about your snake. It's for a project. Can we come and see it?'

'OK.'

Declan led the way upstairs. 'Is this for school?' he asked.

'Sort of,' I said.

Declan opened the door to his bedroom. I wasn't quite sure what to expect. I thought there might be a giant python (or boa constrictor) coiled around his bed. But the only things on his bed were a duvet, a pillow, and a special display case with his best Yu-Gi-Oh! cards.

Then I saw the fish tank. Well, I suppose you'd have to call it a snake tank, because that's what was in it.

'Come over to my vivarium.'

'Is it safe?' I asked.

I was worried in case Jennifer had a panic attack.

'Of course it's safe,' said Jennifer.

We gathered round the snake tank – I mean, vivarium. It contained a dried-up

branch from a tree, and there was a little wooden house in one corner. Oh, and there was a snake in there.

The snake had green and brown and white blotches in a complicated wiggly pattern on its back. And it kept putting out its tongue, flicker, flicker, flicker.

'Want to touch it?'

'No!' I answered, maybe a bit too quickly. I was speaking on behalf of Jennifer and Noah. I didn't want them to run out screaming.

'I'd love to,' said Jennifer.

Declan reached into the tank and put his hand under Ray Quasar. The snake began to coil around his wrist. He lifted it out. It raised its head and looked me right in the eye – trying to work out if I would taste nice, I expect.

Jennifer stretched out her hand, and Declan touched her fingers and the snake wriggled from him to her.

'It's beautiful,' she said. 'Can I stroke it?'

'Sure.'

'Hey, it's lovely and dry. Not even a bit slimy.'

I was getting annoyed about all this. We'd come here to ask serious questions, not to get all kissy-kissy, lovey-dovey over a dangerous predator who might be busy digesting dogs, cats and parrots even as we spoke.

'What kind of snake is it?' I asked. 'A python?'

'A boa constrictor.'

'I thought so. And what does it eat, eh? Warm-blooded animals, I expect. Little furry creatures? Big furry creatures? And other creatures with feathers? Isn't that right?'

Before Declan could answer Jennifer dragged me to one side, using the hand that wasn't holding Ray Quasar.

'You don't still believe that this cute little snake ate all those other animals?' she whispered.

'Yes, well, it might have. Look, I drew some drawings – I meant to show you earlier on.'

I took out the pictures I'd done of the elephant, pig and dog inside the snake.

The one with the elephant fell on the floor. Declan picked it up. He'd been quite well behaved up till then, not acting at all loony, but he made up for that now by running around the room laughing like a maniac.

'Snakes don't eat elephants, you idiot,' he shouted.

'I know they don't. And anyway, no elephants have disappeared, not lately. That was just the first picture. But look at these.

Snakes eat pigs and dogs, see? And it so happens that some dogs and cats – although not, so far, pigs – *have* disappeared. And I think we both know where.'

Then I pointed in a dramatic way at Ray Quasar's tummy.

The dramatic pointing business didn't have exactly the effect I'd been counting on. I'd been hoping that Declan would break down, sobbing, and admit that Ray Quasar was the murderer and that he was the accomplice.

What happened was more or less the exact opposite of that.

The earlier bout of running around and laughing was nothing compared with this. And when he got bored with running, he tried some jumping up and down on the bed, and then some rolling around on the floor.

It was time I took charge again.

'Just laughing like a baboon isn't the same as answering the question.'

'What's the question?'

'Did Ray Quasar eat Trixie – that's Mrs Cake's Jack Russell terrier – plus two other dogs whose names I can't remember, plus Catty the fat, er, I mean, Fatty the cat, and Potty the parrot?'

Declan worked hard to get his face under control. Yes, he was very close to cracking. The case was almost closed.

'Hello, anyone home?' he said, knocking on my head with his knuckles. 'Ray Quasar doesn't eat pigs, or dogs, or cats, or elephants. He's too small. When he's fully grown, he'll 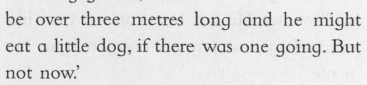 be over three metres long and he might eat a little dog, if there was one going. But not now.'

'What does he eat then?'

I'd noticed that he hadn't mentioned parrots.

'Mice.'

'Mice?'

'Yes, mice. Baby mice. Want to watch?'

'Not really.'

'Yeah, cool.'

That was Jennifer. She was still holding Ray Quasar, although you could equally say that he was holding her. I half hoped that the snake would attack her, and maybe swallow her down to the waist so I could rescue her from the jaws of the beast, like Tarzan. That would show her how brave I was, as well as going a long way to proving the snake's guilt. After all, if you'd eat a girl like that, then you'd eat anything – dogs, cats, mushy peas, Brussels sprouts, anything.

But sadly he didn't try to strangulate and swallow her. He just hung on her arm like a handbag and put his nasty tongue out at me.

'Actually it's feeding time now. I've got

some mice defrosting in the fridge next to the yogurt. Hang on here and I'll get them.'

Then he ran out of the room.

'How do you think the interrogation's going?' I said to my Elite Force, after a pause.

'Quite good,' said Noah, looking down at his feet.

'Rubbish, actually,' said Jennifer.

Obviously she'd taken over the family role of moaner.

'How can you say that when we're about to see Ray Quasar eat a baby mouse?'

'Well, I admit that will be quite interesting.'

'One thing, though,' said Noah. 'If Ray Quasar eats the mice, can we rule him out of our enquiries?'

I thought for a moment.

'Well, yes, we can.'

'Hooray,' said Jennifer sarcastically.

'In an investigation you often make an advance by eliminating suspects.'

Ray Quasar ate the mice.

Four little pink baby mice.

He wrapped himself around them, giving them a good old constrict even though they were already so dead they'd been in the freezer for six months. Then he swallowed them.

It's a strange world in which eating four little tiny pink baby mice means you are innocent. But we don't get a choice. This is the only world we have. So I declared Ray Quasar the boa constrictor Not Guilty, and we went home.

But not before Declan gave Jennifer a present – a nasty dried-up old snakeskin that Ray Quasar had grown out of. The way she smiled and blushed you'd have thought it was a diamond ring.

Chapter 12

BRAINSTORMING

I had more pondering to do that night. So I was awake yet again when I heard the sound of Rude Word being dragged out of the garage and tied up to the gate post. I didn't even bother to look.

The next morning I brought Rude Word out some Weetabix. He wasn't there. I looked under the blankets in his baby bath. No sign.

'Dad, where's Rudy?' I asked when I came back into the kitchen.

My dad looked at my mum. My mum looked at the ceiling. You wouldn't have thought that ceilings were that interesting.

'Isn't he outside?' she said.

'No, I've just looked. I was bringing him his Weetabix.'

'Oh no,' said Dad, in a dramatic kind of way, 'do you think it's another of those mysterious disappearances?'

'That must be it,' said Mum, still looking very closely at the ceiling. She was obviously going to be a world expert on ceilings. 'What shall we do?'

This was terrible. It was the worst thing that had happened to me ever in my life. My lovable pet had been snatched. Something horrible was probably eating him right now.

'You've got to phone the police,' I yelled. 'And the army. And the RAF. They can send out helicopter gunships.'

Just then there was a screech of tyres outside on the road. I ran to the window, hoping there might be a small crash to see – I don't mean a bad one with blood, but just one with maybe a dent in the bumper, or a knocked-down lamppost. All I saw was the back of a car driving away at probably about two hundred miles an hour. And something else. A friendly brown-and-black face, pushing its way through our front gate.

'Rudy's back,' I yelled. 'Rudy's back!'

'Oh,' said Dad, 'how nice. He must have just gone off for a walk.'

'Yippee,' said Mum, but not in the way you usually say yippee – more in the way you'd say, 'Guess what, my granny died.'

Sometimes grown-ups can be quite hard to understand.

Anyway, I ran out and hugged Rudy and then went to school.

There was high drama at school. As soon as I got in through the school gates I could tell that Declan wasn't in a happy mood. He was sitting on one of the benches with his head in his hands. Normally at this time he'd be charging around the playground shouting, 'Bananas,' at the top of his voice. There was a group of children around him, mainly the Commando Gang, but also a few other kids who were probably hanging around in the hope that Declan would do something loony.

'What's wrong?' I asked.

Declan just shook his head.

'It's Ray Quasar.'

That was Nicky speaking. He was one of the nice boys at school, and hardly ever called anyone names or made fun of them unless they asked for it. He was also the best at gymnastics, except for Jenny, and he could do a handstand for the whole of morning break, unless someone pushed him over, which happened quite a lot.

'What about Ray Quasar?'

'He's vanished. Escaped or something. Declan got up this morning and he wasn't in his tank. He's too upset to even talk. He hasn't shouted "Bananas" once.'

'Blimey.'

Another victim. The pet-eater was moving on to reptiles now, and a suspect had become a victim.

It was time for action. I found the Bare Bum Gang and called a Special Emergency Gang Meeting, to be held in the den after tea. To make sure everyone came, I said we could have two sweets each out of our sweet stash.

I brought my biggest drawing pad and some felt tips. I also brought ten broken pencils and a pencil sharpener. And two torches, because it was beginning to get dark in the evenings. I needed all those things because I'd decided we had to have a brainstorming session. That is when you have to solve a problem and the first thing you do is write down everything that comes into your head, and then you get rid of the silly things, and what you have left is the answer.

I brought Rudy with me and tied him up outside to guard the entrance.

I was in charge of the pad and the pens. The broken pencils and the pencil sharpener were for Jamie, because he needed something to do while we were brainstorming. Jamie was only the fifth best in the Gang at pencil sharpening, after me, Noah, Jenny and The Moan, but he usually managed to sharpen the right end, and hardly ever shoved a pencil so far up his nose he had

to go to hospital to have it removed.

When we'd all finished our sweets, I began.

'Right,' I said. 'Now, we know that we are dealing with something very evil indeed – probably the most evil thing that has ever existed. More evil than Dracula or a giant clam that grabs you under the water and then drowns you and then slowly dissolves

your flesh while you're still alive.'

There was a gasp from the Gang.

'And,' I continued, 'we've also eliminated the two chief suspects from our investigation – Rude Word and Ray Quasar. That leaves us back at square one: just who, or what, is eating our pets? Ideas please, gentlemen, and Jennifer as well – you count as a gentleman, for the sake of this meeting.'

'Gee, thanks,' she said.

'Right then, other suspects – fire away.'

So this is the list of suspects we came up with (I won't say who had most of the best ideas because that would be boasting):

- A tiger
- A lion
- A leopard (or panther)
- A jaguar
- A puma
- A wolf
- A bear (polar, black or grizzly)

- A new kind of giant badger, so far unknown to science
- A crocodile (or alligator)
- Aliens;
- Evil people (e.g. cannibals)
- Starving people (e.g. cannibals who haven't eaten anyone for ages)
- A shark (e.g. great white, tiger, hammer-head, etc., etc.)
- A killer whale
- A T. Rex
- A velociraptor
- King Kong

'That's a brilliant list,' I said. 'Now we'll do the second part, which is getting rid of the rubbish ones. Then whatever is left is clearly the culprit.' I added in a whisper to Jamie, 'The culprit means the one that did it.'

But Jamie was too busy sharpening the pencils to notice.

Getting rid of the rubbish ones was quite

easy. We began with those that lived in other countries, which eliminated the tiger, lion, leopard, jaguar, puma, wolf and bear. Then we got rid of the ones that mainly hunted in the water, which meant the various types of shark, the killer whale and the crocodile (or alligator). Then we dumped the ones that were extinct, i.e. the T. Rex and velociraptor, because everyone knows that the movie *Jurassic Park* is just made up, except for Jamie who believes everything on the telly is true.

Then we got rid of the cannibals, because cannibals eat people and not pets, and anyway, they usually live in the jungle or on an island.

That left the aliens and King Kong.

'I was only joking about King Kong,' said Jennifer.

'What do you mean, joking? We're not messing about here, you know. This is a matter of life and death.'

'I said it because of all the stupid ones

that you said, like jaguars and T. Rexes.'

'Fine,' I continued. 'We'll scratch King Kong off the list. Anyway, I knew it wasn't him, because he got riddled with machine-gun bullets on top of the Empire State Building. That just leaves the aliens.'

There was a shocked silence after that, as the Bare Bum Gang thought about the terrible foe we were up against.

Then Jamie did one of his famous gigantic burps. I haven't mentioned Jamie's famous gigantic burps before, partly because I find them disgusting, and partly because I forgot to. They were so loud they didn't sound human, more like the sound a machine would make, a bit like an electric drill combined with a jet fighter taking off. Jamie was definitely the best at doing gigantic burps, though The Moan was slightly better at farting, which is also disgusting, especially in enclosed spaces such as dens and the International Space Station.

It's quite hard writing down how a burp (or a fart) sounds, but if I had to try it would be like this:

GGGGRRRRROOOOOOOOOOOUUUUUUUU-UURRRRRRRRRRRRPP.

Naturally we all looked round at him, not sure whether this was the alarm signal for being attacked (maybe even by the same aliens we'd already identified as the pet murderers), or just one of his ordinary burps.

Throughout all this Jamie carried on sharpening the pencils – interestingly, burping is one of those things you can do while you carry on doing something else, unlike farting or tying your shoe laces, which are things you have to do all by themselves. Then Jamie stopped sharpening.

'I don't think it's aliens,' he said.

'Well, who cares what you think, Mr Smelly Burper?' said Jennifer.

'Actually, Jennifer,' I said, 'everyone is allowed to say what they think in this gang, even if they do disgusting burps. So go on,

Jamie. Why do you think it's not aliens eating the pets?'

'Well, I think the mistake you've made is to think that something must be eating the animals.'

'But how else can they be disappearing?'

'Eating isn't the only way of disappearing something, you know, Ludo.'

'Oh, so now you're saying it's magic? Very likely.'

That was The Moan, being sarcastic again.

'No,' Jamie replied calmly. 'I think they've been stolen.'

'By aliens?'

'No, by people.'

'What for?'

'To sell. For money. To other people who want pets.'

Then Jamie went back to sharpening the pencils. He'd done eight by that time.

The rest of us looked at each other.

Noah was the first one to speak.

'He's got it, hasn't he? We've been barking up the wrong tree all this time. Nothing's eating the animals – they're being stolen. It's only the fancy pets that have gone, the ones they can sell for a lot of money.'

'You know what, Jamie?' I said.

'What?'

'You're brilliant. In fact, that was such a good idea, I've decided that you're not the stupidest person in the Bare Bum Gang any more.'

Jamie pulled a strange face, as if he wasn't sure whether to be happy or annoyed. There's no pleasing some people.

'Well, who is then?' asked Jennifer.

'Mmm,' I said. 'Let's see. Well, it can't be me, because I'm the Leader. And it's not you, because you're on the top table for everything.' Jennifer smiled a big smile. 'And Noah, you're quite clever, except at spelling.' Noah looked reasonably happy with that. 'So, it must be you, Moan, I'm afraid.'

'No way! That's so unfair!'

'Look, don't make a fuss about it. Jamie never minded being the stupidest. He just got on with it and then had his good idea. I suggest that you try harder, and then you can climb up the rankings.'

'I'm going home,' he said.

'Well, you can if you like, but that means you won't be invited on the best bit of this whole adventure,' I said.

'Oh? What's that then?'

'The part where we solve the crime.'

Chapter 13

THE HUNT BEGINS

Solving the crime had to wait until Saturday. By that stage two more cats and three dogs had gone, along with a tank full of tropical fish.

We arranged to meet at the den at zero nine-thirty hundred hours o'clock, which is half past nine. Well, we sort of arranged to meet at zero nine-thirty hundred hours o'clock, but then I remembered that there was still quite good children's telly on then, so we changed it to ten hundred hours o'clock.

I phoned the others and told them to come

in disguise, because we were secret agents on a mission.

For my disguise I wore a pair of my mum's sunglasses and a balaclava. And I brought my plastic binoculars, a magnifying glass and my spud gun, along with a potato for ammunition. In case you haven't seen one, a spud gun is a gun which fires potato bullets. You have to be careful because they can blind you if you fire it into your eye at short range. Although I suppose you'd have to fire it into both eyes, one after the other, to blind yourself properly, and you'd have to be pretty silly to do that.

I made a mental note not to let Jamie play with the spud gun, even though he was no longer officially the stupidest member of the Gang.

Rudy looked up at me from Ivy's old bath.

'Come on, boy,' I said.

Yes, at long last he was going to earn his place in the Bare Bum Gang.

I realized my mistake when I saw the others waiting for me at the den. I should have explained that the disguise was so that we didn't stand out. But they would have stood out less if they'd been carrying a huge banner with LOOK AT ME written on it in letters three metres tall.

Noah, who really should have known better, was wearing his Spider-Man costume. The Moan was dressed as a spaceman and Jamie had a cowboy outfit, with a giant cowboy hat, a waistcoat with a silver sheriff's badge, flapping leather trousers and a gun-belt with two toy pistols. But Jenny was the worst. She had on a pink fairy costume, complete with wings. At least she didn't have the wand.

'What are you lot playing at?' I yelled in desperation.

Noah looked bewildered. 'You said to come in fancy dress.'

'I did not. I said *in disguise.*'

'I'm sure you said fancy dress.'

'Didn't.'

'Did.'

That could have gone on for hours, but we had work to do.

'Doesn't matter now. Jenny, did you bring it?'

'My wand?'

'No, not your wand. The *thing*.'

'Yes, of course I brought it, I'm not a dummy. But you'd better be careful with it. It was a present to me.'

She reached into her fairy costume. The thing she pulled out looked, for a second, in its shimmeriness, like part of the costume. It was the snakeskin she'd been given by Declan. I took it and crouched down in front of Rudy.

'Here, boy. Come snuffle this.'

Rudy instantly waddled over and went into hyper-snuffle mode. He was definitely excited about the snakeskin.

Then, before I could stop him, he sucked

it into his slobbery mouth, gave it a quick chew, and then swallowed it down, the way you would a slice of bacon. All that was left in my hand was the last bit of skin from the back end of the snake.

Unfortunately Jennifer saw it all.

'You beast!' she screamed, and aimed a big kick at Rudy.

At least that's what I thought she was doing. She was actually aiming a big kick at me. It landed on my bottom and I went sprawling face first on the ground.

It's always embarrassing when someone kicks you up the bum and you end up flat on your face. It's doubly embarrassing when the thing doing the kicking is a big pink fairy.

I thought about kicking her back, but decided not to for three reasons:

1. It's wrong to kick girls.
2. Jennifer was allowed to be upset because her present had been eaten by Rudy.

3. We had to get on with the mission.

Oh, and:

4. She'd only kick me again, even harder.

'I'm sorry about the snakeskin, Jenny,' I said. 'But there's something more important going on here. There's a real snake to save, along with other nice pets.'

I think the others were actually quite impressed with my behaviour. Sometimes being a Great Leader involves getting kicked up the bum by a fairy and rising above it to save kidnapped parrots, snakes, fat cats, etc.

I took Rudy's ugly face in my hands.

'OK, boy,' I said. 'Listen like you've never listened before.' I dangled the last bit of snakeskin before his snuffly nose and said, 'Find, Rudy, Find.'

Rudy looked up at me, his milky eyes trying hard to understand. I felt the Gang watching closely. If this didn't work, there

was no way I could carry on as its Great
Leader.

Come on, Rudy, I begged silently.

Then there was a little wag from his tail,
and his mouth opened into an eager grin.
He heaved himself up and began to trundle
off in the direction of the park.

'It's working!' I yelled. 'Follow Rudy,
everyone.'

Chapter 14

THE HUNT CONTINUES

It was lucky that Rudy wasn't one of the fastest dogs, because then he'd have been out of sight in no time. Even a medium-paced dog would have been too much for us to keep up with. But Rudy didn't really run at all. He moved with a sort of rolling waddle, with a bit of staggering thrown in. So we jogged along with him quite easily.

We reached the park, and then went across the waste ground beyond it, and then past the sewage works, and then through some back gardens, and then through some front gardens. By that stage we were deep in enemy territory, by which I mean the New Estate, where our old rivals the Dockery Gang lived. But they weren't around. They were probably watching telly or mugging old ladies while we were saving the world. No one saw us, which was lucky, considering how silly the others looked. I mean the cowboy, the astronaut, Spider-Man and the fairy.

I was very impressed with Rudy. He just went straight on, never turning his head, never changing pace. He was like a small, podgy, ugly, hairy guided missile.

He must really have liked the taste of that snakeskin.

Past the New Estate it gets a bit creepy. There are some low concrete buildings there and no one even knows what they're for. Then you get to lots of lock-up garages, hardly any of them with cars in, and it always seems dim and dingy, even on a sunny morning.

Finally Rudy came to a row of garages. There was graffiti written all over the doors, and I don't care how rude the rude word was that we named Rude Word after, I don't believe it was as rude as the rude words we saw there.

'Cover your eyes up, Jennifer,' I said.

I was worried that she might faint if she read the really rude words. That can happen to girls sometimes, especially if they get over-excited, or put knickers on from last year that are too small for them and cut off the circulation to their brains.

'Cover your own up!' she replied.

But there wasn't time for an argument, because Rudy had homed in on one of the garages. He stuck his nose into the gap at the bottom of the door, as if he was trying to squeeze under it. There was a big padlock on the door.

'This is it,' I said.

'I can't hear anything,' said The Moan, pressing his ear to the door.

'I think there are windows at the back —

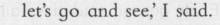

let's go and see,' I said.

I dragged Rudy with me, but he really wanted to stay snuffling at the door.

There was an allotment at the back of the garages. Allotments are supposed to be where old men in flat caps grow their vegetables, but this was pretty manky, as allotments go. There was nothing there you'd want to eat — just old prams, broken bottles, sheds that looked like they'd been bombed in the war and left for dead, and lots and lots of weeds. Oh, and some Brussels sprouts.

'It's horrible back here,' said The Moan.

You couldn't argue with that.

The garage we were looking for was right in the middle of the row, but from behind it was hard to work out which one it was. Each garage had a small window at the back, most of them grimy and dusty and covered in cobwebs. They were too high to see through, so I had to get Jamie to lift me up. The first one I looked in was empty. The next had rolls of carpet right up to the ceiling. The third window was so dusty and filthy I could hardly see through.

'A bit higher,' I said to Jamie.

He grunted and lifted me higher.

'Anything there?' asked Jennifer.

'Can't . . . make . . . it . . . out.'

'Glasses,' said Noah.

'What?'

'You've still got the sunglasses on. It's why you can't see.'

'Oh yes.'

I put the sunglasses in my pocket.

'Bozo,' said The Moan.

'Get down, dog,' shouted Jamie.

I looked down and saw Rudy jumping up. This must be the right one.

I peered again. It was definitely better without the sunglasses. There seemed to be wooden boxes. I strained through the gloom. There was chicken wire in front of the boxes. Then I saw a pale glint in the darkness.

An eye. A sad eye, looking out at me. Then more. Hundreds of them.

'Yes,' I hissed, 'it's them! It's the pets!'

Chapter 15

THE RESCUE

I climbed down, nearly falling into a patch of nettles. Then Jamie had to help the others get up to see, while I patted Rudy and told him what a good boy he was.

'I actually think you've got something right for a change,' said The Moan.

'What shall we do now?' asked Noah.

I did some quick thinking.

'Easy. We've got to rescue them. We'll be famous. I expect we'll be on the telly, and there's probably a huge reward, maybe a million pounds.'

'Really?' said Noah hopefully.

'No way,' said The Moan. 'A hundred pounds at the most.'

Then we had a long discussion about how much the reward would be. In the end we decided it would be £18,000. Then we realized it was a really hard sum to divide £18,000 by four, so we decided we would settle for £16,000, which was £4,000 each.

'But how are we going to rescue them?' said Noah when the finances had been sorted out.

'I'm going in,' I said, sounding incredibly brave, I thought. 'Then I'll hand them out, one at a time.'

I searched around until I found an old crate to stand on, which was much better than having Jamie huffing and puffing with me on his shoulders. Back at the window I could see light seeping through a crack in the garage door. The cages were all around the walls, piled on top of each other. There must have been thirty or forty of them.

I realized that this was a major pet-smuggling operation, probably controlled by the Mafia, the Triads or the Jacuzzi. You've probably heard of the Mafia, and the Triads are like them except from China, and the Jacuzzi are like them but from Japan. The Jacuzzi have tattoos all over their bodies and they chop you up with Samurai swords if you forget to bow to them in the right way.

I poked my finger around the window to see if I could open it. It didn't budge. Then I tried to remember if there was anything in my book of *How to Be a Spy* about opening windows, but I came up blank. What I needed was the book of *How to Be a Burglar*.

So I got down off the crate and found half a brick.

'You can't!' said Noah. 'It's vandalism.'

'Go on,' said The Moan. 'It's an adventure.'

Jennifer gave me a quick nod.

Jamie picked his nose, looked at the bogey, thought about eating it, then flicked it away. He was definitely becoming more civilized.

I paused for a moment to think over the rights and wrongs of what I was about to do. Then I smashed the window.

Now, obviously, as Noah was trying to say, smashing windows is one of the naughtiest things you can do – much, much worse than weeing on the toilet seat or hiding your granny's false teeth. But this was for a good cause, saving animals from deadly peril, etc., etc., and besides, it's always fun to break glass.

The sound should have got the animals excited. But apart from one small meow, a single bark, and what might have been a hiss, they didn't make much noise.

'They've been drugged,' I said.

It was then that I heard voices coming from the other side of the garage door.

'Sshhh!' I whispered to the others. 'They're here!'

'Who?'

'The baddies.'

I ducked down below the level of the window and froze. I couldn't quite make out what they were saying, but they sounded gruff and rough and definitely Japanese.

It was the Jacuzzi hitmen for sure!

Suddenly the door was wrenched open with a loud scraping noise. I peeped one eye over the window frame. I saw two figures outlined against the bright sky. One of them was holding something fluffy by its long ears.

A bunny!

'That's right,' said one. 'Shove it in that cage there.'

He didn't sound *very* Japanese, but you never know for sure. Then there was exactly the sound you'd expect to hear if a big rabbit was being pushed into a small cage.

'That's the lot,' said another voice. 'I reckon we've got every decent pedigree pet in this town. Must be at least five grand's worth of cat, dog, parrot and rabbit in here.'

'Yeah,' said the first voice. 'Time to shift 'em. Let's go and get the van.'

They scraped the door shut behind them.

I jumped down and told the others what I'd heard.

'We haven't got long,' I said. 'And this could be dangerous. Highly dangerous. Like playing with fire while you're holding two sticks of dynamite and you're suspended over a live volcano with a tidal wave coming.'

Jamie's mouth opened. Even Jennifer looked impressed.

I continued: 'We don't know who's been stealing these animals, but I think we can safely say that they're not very nice people. Who knows what they'll do if they catch us here.'

I didn't mention Samurai swords or getting sliced up like salami.

'Anyone got a mobile phone?' I asked.

They all shook their heads.

'My dad says they give you brain cancer,' said Noah.

'My mum thinks they're common,' said Jenny.

'OK. In that case we have to run and get help. Right, Moan, you and Jennifer go and phone the police from the phone box on the High Street.'

'It always smells of wee in there,' said Jennifer.

'You'll have to put up with the smell of wee this once. Tell the police it's a double emergency and they have to come right away, even if they've got another job to do, like chasing bank robbers.'

They both nodded.

'Jamie, you don't live far from here — can you run home and get your dad to come?'

'You bet,' he said.

Jamie's dad looked like Frankenstein's monster, but he was actually very nice and a big softy.

'Tell him to bring his cricket bat,' I added.

'What about me?' asked Noah.

'You and me are going to try to rescue as many pets as we can, in case the police and Jamie's dad don't make it in time.'

'That's so brave,' said Jennifer.

'Well, not really,' I said modestly.

'Seems stupid to me,' said The Moan, but that was to be expected from him. 'It isn't a job for kids. You should come with us.'

'Pah,' I said. 'Running away is for cowards. OK, let's synchronize watches.'

'Why?' said The Moan.

'Because you're supposed to. It's now ten thirty-five oh hundred hours o'clock precisely. Jamie, that means the little hand is pointing to the—'

'I know,' said Jamie, quite crossly.

I got out my spud gun and the potato and loaded up.

'Be careful,' said Jennifer, and kissed my cheek. Normally, of course, I would have had to wipe it off. But as this was a special occasion I left it there. I gave her a quick, brave smile, and then said, 'OK then – go, go, go, and good luck on your missions.'

Chapter 16

THE CATCH

Noah, Rudy and I watched the others run away in various directions across the allotments.

'Just us, now,' I said.

I put the loaded spud gun back in my pocket and climbed onto the crate. With the glass broken I could put my arm through (very carefully, as broken glass can kill you as easily as a nuclear explosion).

I flipped the catch and the window creaked open. I heaved up onto the window-sill and then jumped down into the dark garage.

It was pretty smelly in there. The pet-snatchers hadn't bothered to take the animals outside for walkies (or flyies – in the case of the parrot), so they'd all had to do their poos in their cages.

I looked in each of the cages. There were all kinds of fancy dogs, the sort you see posh ladies carrying around in their handbags. There were beautiful fluffy cats, any one of which might have been Fatty the Persian. There were two parrots, one grey one and another that looked like it had been painted by a little kid determined to use every colour in his paint box. I wasn't sure which one was Potty. I tried saying, 'Hello, Potty,' to each of them, to see if they'd answer back, but they just looked at me like I was mad.

I found Trixie. I put my fingers through the wire and she tried to bite them off. Some things don't change. And in the next cage there was good old Ray Quasar, boa constrictor (or was it python?). He stuck his tongue out at me in a friendly way.

'Hurry up.'

That was Noah outside, sounding anxious.

I picked up a cage with a cat in it. It was heavier than I expected. I carried it over to the window. I'd forgotten that the window was so high. I stretched up and balanced the cat cage on the ledge.

'Here,' I said.

I saw two hands reach up and take the cage.

We got two more cages out, one with a small yappy dog

and the other with the bunny rabbit.

But then I heard the sound I'd been dreading – the sound of the thieves' van pulling up outside. Noah heard it too.

'Get out of there,' he hissed.

I ran to the window. I stretched and stretched, but it was too high to climb out of. My heart was racing and sweat poured down my face, making my balaclava all clammy.

'I can't reach it,' I said to Noah. 'Run away and save yourself.'

'But . . .'

'That's an order.'

I knew then that I had only one chance. I ran around the garage banging on the tops of all the cages, trying to get the still half-drugged animals riled up. The dogs started barking, the cats spitting, the snake hissing, the parrots squawking.

'What a racket,' I heard one of the pet-robbers say. Then I head the grating sound of someone trying to open the padlock. I had just a few seconds more. I flicked open the little catches on the cages and opened the doors.

There was one that took a bit of nerve to reach inside.

The garage door was being dragged back. Full dazzling light hit my eyes.

It was now or never.

With a yell I kicked over as many cages as I could, sending cats and dogs and parrots leaping and flying in all directions. Then, with a mighty effort, I hurled the long, heavy body of Ray Quasar at the shape of the first man. Then I did a quick draw with my spud gun and fired it in the face of the one behind him.

At the same moment I leaped forwards. I was at the heart of a snarling, snapping mass of angry animal flesh. And Trixie was doing more than her fair share of snapping. Good doggie!

I saw the startled look on the face of the man just before the snake hit him. Ray Quasar wrapped himself round the man's

neck and shoulders as he fell back. The second man also staggered back, hit right on the end of his nose by the spud bullet.

There was a space for me to escape through. If I could only slip past them I knew that I could get away.

I was out of the door, almost there, almost free. Then I felt a hand reach out and grab the back of my balaclava. I ducked and

squirmed and the balaclava came off in the man's hand. But I had slowed down, and now he moved to block the way.

It was the one I'd hit on the nose with the spud gun. He wasn't a Japanese Jacuzzi after all, but just an ordinary man in a tracksuit top and jeans. There were still animals milling around, but they weren't the threatening pack that they'd first been when they burst out of their cages.

The man didn't look very happy, but at least he wasn't wrestling with a metre-long snake like his friend, so he should have been thanking his lucky stars, if you ask me.

'You little thug,' he said.

'I'm not a thug,' I yelled back. 'You're the baddies here, not me, and you're going to get it.'

Brave words, but I didn't feel brave. I felt

more frightened than I'd ever felt in my life before. The man just chuckled.

Then I saw something that cheered me up by at least a thousand per cent.

'Get them, boy!'

The man spun round.

It was Noah and Rudy. They hadn't run away; they'd just gone round to the front of the garages.

Noah, looking rather striking in his Spider-Man costume, was pointing at the man, urging Rudy to attack, to prove once and for all that he was a true member of the Bare Bum Gang. Rudy growled menacingly, a look of hate in his eyes.

And then he sat down and appeared to go to sleep.

'Ha, not much of a mutt. That's why we threw him out of the car.'

'That was ...'

It was all falling into place.

'So then, what shall we do with the two of you?'

But just then Trixie reappeared. She quickly sized up the situation, deciding who to bite first.

I then had my first piece of good luck in ages. Instead of attacking me, she fastened onto the man's trousers, snarling and growling in the best Trixie way.

The man said some very rude words. Perhaps that's what woke Rudy up – I mean, hearing his real name shouted out like that. But once he was awake he saw the man give Trixie a big kick, sending the poor little dog flying through the air.

Finally Rudy was moved to anger. And in a flash I realized that Rudy hadn't chased Trixie to eat her, but because he loved her and wanted to marry her. And now, with a fearsome roar, he charged at the man.

Kicking little rats is one thing, but facing up to a big fat dog like Rude Word is quite another, and the man turned to run.

Now, anyone knows that if you turn your back on a charging dog only one thing is going to happen. And that happened now. Rudy took a massive bite out of the man's bum. I heard the wet sound of his teeth sinking into the man's wobbly buttock.

His scream sounded like this:

'AAAEEEEEIIIIIIIIOOOOOOOUUUUUU.'

It was as if he was trying to yell out all the vowels in the right order. I was quite impressed that he got it right, considering there was a dog attached to his bottom.

Noah ran towards me, grabbed my arm and yelled at me to run.

'No need,' I said, and pointed along the row of garages. Jamie's dad was coming, armed not just with his cricket bat, but with the pads and helmet as well. And right behind him, its nee-naw blaring loudly, came the police car.

'I don't think we've anything to worry about here, Noah,' I said, sounding like a cool secret agent who's just defeated the super-villains without even breaking into a sweat.

Chapter 17

GROUNDED

I did actually have something to worry about.

It was a day later and I was standing in our living room. The telly wasn't on, which is usually a sign that something terrible is happening.

'What you did was very dangerous and irresponsible. I think that your parents should ground you for at least a week. And I believe they agree with me.'

A very fat police sergeant with at least eight quivering chins was giving me a big telling off.

'You could have got yourself into a very tricky situation. If we hadn't arrived that minute, I don't know what would have happened.'

At that minute, I wanted to tell him, one of the men was trying to extract Rudy from his bottom, and the other was being strangled (but not to death) by Ray Quasar. I thought we were fairly safe.

Anyway, the three policemen in the car arrested the pet thieves. They told us later that they'd been on their trail as they moved around stealing animals and selling them to pet shops, who sold them on again to ordinary people. Most of the animals were recovered, except for the parrots, which flew away together for ever and probably got married, like Trixie and Rudy.

Back in our living room, my mum said, 'I hope you're listening to the policeman, Ludo. We were worried sick.'

Well, that wasn't true either. They didn't even know I was in danger until after it happened, and they knew I was safe now.

Then my dad joined in. 'I think you owe us all an apology.'

So much for the £16,000 reward!

But there was no point arguing.

'Sorry,' I said.

Then my mum and dad hugged me and the fat policemen went away.

'Am I really grounded?'

'Well,' said my dad, 'you stayed in last night, so we'll say you've served your sentence.'

'Thanks, Dad.'

'It was really brave,' he said. 'Just very silly.'

I nodded. It was very silly.

The whole gang met up that evening in the den.

'I think that's the best adventure we've ever had,' said Jamie.

We all agreed.

'And it was all thanks to Rudy,' Noah said.

'It would have been even better if he'd found the treasure,' said The Moan.

'Oh, we've got all our lives to find treasure,' I said, 'but we can only have adventures when we're kids.'

Then Jennifer did something very, very strange.

She kissed me on the cheek again.

'Any more of that,' I said, blushing, 'and you're out of the Bare Bum Gang for good.'

And then we were all laughing, and we didn't stop until it was time to go home.

You're probably wondering where Rudy was. Well, I'm going to have to take you back again to those garages.

The baddies were bundled into the back of the police car, and two of the policemen were trying to round up the escaped animals. Then I noticed that Ray Quasar wasn't around. And nor was Rudy.

Noah and I started to look for them. Then I heard a horrible crunching noise. It seemed to be coming from underneath the pet-stealer's van. We crouched down to look. The sight was even more horrible than the sound. Rudy and Trixie were both there. Along with Ray Quasar. Rudy was eating his way down Ray Quasar from the top, and Trixie was eating her way up from the bottom. They were about to meet in the middle.

Declan never found out what happened to his snake, which was probably a good thing. I let him think that Ray Quasar had escaped into the sewer, where he would grow to an enormous size and eventually burst out of someone's toilet one day and eat them. That cheered him up. And I thought the least I could do was to let him share Rudy. The agreement was that Declan would look after Rudy all year except for the summer holidays, when he would come and stay with us. He seemed quite happy with that arrangement. They both did.

And so did my mum and dad.